Mystery Mansion

Phil Roxbee Cox

Adapted by Jane Bingham

Illustrated by
Sue Hellard

Reading Consultant: Alison Kelly
University of Surrey Roehampton

Contents

Chapter 1

The horror begins

It was a cold winter's night in the village of Nether Bogey. Loud moans rang out from Mystery Mansion, deep in the marshes, and a glowing, yellow mist curled around its walls.

3

Down in the gloomy churchyard,
Jimmy Flint was digging graves.
He shivered when he heard the
moans, but he kept on digging.

For a moment, Jimmy wished
he was home in bed. Then he
remembered his nightmares.

Almost every night, Jimmy dreamed a savage wolf was chasing him. He stopped digging and nervously looked up. He had the feeling something was watching him now.

Jimmy wiped his sweaty face with a rag. Then, gripping his shovel tightly, he began to dig even faster.

A few minutes later, Jimmy heard a noise. He turned around slowly... to see a dark shape springing out of the bushes at him.

Jimmy let out a piercing yell. His worst nightmare had just come true.

Chapter 2

Harry's adventure

Sounds like the master's in a rage again.

Life was hard for the servants at Mystery Mansion. The ancient house was cold and crumbling and everyone was scared of the master, Lord Rakenhell. Ever since his son Edmund had left, ten years earlier, his bad temper had grown worse.

7

They were even more scared of the butler, Mr. Paulfrey – the most important servant in the house. The least important servant, according to Mr. Paulfrey, was Harry Grubb.

Harry's main job was cleaning all the boots and shoes but, however hard he tried, he could never please the butler.

Scrub faster, Grubb!

In all of Mystery Mansion,
Harry liked only two people. One
was Anna, the dusting maid, and
the other was Miss Charlotte,
Lord Rakenhell's only daughter.

Harry was great friends with
Anna, but he had never dared
speak to Miss Charlotte.

One bitterly cold December day, the cook sent Harry with a message for the gamekeeper. On the way, he passed a blazing fire. He was just warming his hands over the flames, when a voice barked at him.

It was Colly, the head gardener.

Harry explained where he was going, but Colly had other plans for him.

"Put this in the hollow tree trunk by the river," he said, handing Harry a small envelope.

Don't tell anyone, now!

Harry raced off. But he hadn't gone far when he heard a cry from the river...

It was Miss Charlotte. She had fallen through the ice and was up to her shoulders in freezing water.

Harry rushed to a fallen tree, broke off a branch and raced back.

Standing firm on the bank, he swung one end of the branch over the river.

"Grab onto this, Miss Charlotte," he shouted, "and I'll pull you out."

In just a few minutes, Charlotte was on the riverbank, shivering and gasping.

You saved my life, Harry. Thank you!

Charlotte was safe, but Harry was worried that she would die of cold. "Follow me, miss," he said. "I know where to find some dry clothes for you."

Before long, they'd reached Colly's shed, where Harry snatched up a bundle of clothes.

Soon, Miss Charlotte was warm and dry, though she felt rather silly.

Harry had other things to worry about. He'd lost Colly's envelope and he still hadn't delivered the message for Cook. He was going to be in big trouble.

Chapter 3

Harry in trouble

Harry ran to the gamekeeper with Cook's message but he couldn't find the envelope anywhere.

Then, running back into the house, he bumped into Mr. Paulfrey — who quickly hid something behind his back.

"Where have you been, Grubb?" the butler snarled.

16

Harry had promised never to tell what happened at the river, so he kept quiet.

"Answer me boy!" Mr. Paulfrey shouted, but Harry simply looked down in silence.

Cat got your tongue?

Paulfrey thought for a moment. Then his mouth twisted into a cruel smile. "Since you don't want to talk to anyone, you can collect up all the boots and shoes and work outside."

Harry worked for hours in the icy courtyard. He sat shaking, his fingers stiff with cold. He was beginning to despair, when he heard someone call him.

Harry looked around and spotted Miss Charlotte.

"Whatever are you doing out there in the cold?" she called. "Come in at once!"

A few minutes later, Harry was thawing out and drinking hot soup beside the kitchen fire.

Thank you, Miss Charlotte!

But he couldn't relax for long. A door burst open and Colly strode into the kitchen. "Well, did you deliver my envelope?" he asked.

"N-no," Harry admitted.

"Harry!" said Colly, turning to go. "I'll just have to find the spare key," he muttered.

Chapter 4

Terror in the tower

The next day, there were four
funerals in Nether Bogey. Three
men had drowned in the nearby
marshes. The fourth man, Jimmy
Flint, had died
of fright.

Why do so
many people die
around here?

After the funeral, Magnus Duggan, the clock winder, slowly climbed the church tower to wind the clock. He was exhausted.

For the last few nights, noises from Mystery Mansion had kept him awake. If he did fall asleep, it was to terrifying nightmares, filled with bats.

Now, as he climbed, Magnus heard strange scuffles overhead.

H-hello?

The next moment, he was surrounded by leathery wings. Hundreds of bats were flapping over his head.

With a terrified scream, Magnus fell back down the stairs... just as he always did in his nightmares.

Chapter 5

Midnight secrets

A few nights later, Harry woke
to find Anna standing by his bed.

"There are strange noises coming
from downstairs," she hissed. "Come
on! Let's see what's happening."

24

Harry was terrified. The servants weren't allowed to leave their rooms at night – and Mr. Paulfrey had told them to ignore any noises they heard. But he couldn't let Anna go down alone.

Are you sure this is a good idea?

"I think the noises were coming from the kitchen," Anna whispered, leading the way.

To Harry's relief, the kitchen was empty. He was about to suggest going back to bed, when Anna spotted a light outside. Peering into the darkness, they saw three shadowy figures.

They're heading for the ruined chapel. Come on!

What if we get caught?

Harry followed Anna into the garden and crouched down behind a pillar in the ruined chapel. From their hiding place, they had a perfect view of the three figures.

One was Mr. Paulfrey. One was Dr. Grimm, the village doctor. And the third was…

...Lord Rakenhell himself! He was barking out orders while Paulfrey dug up lumps of soil and plants.

"What are they doing?" Harry asked Anna. She shrugged.

Suddenly, they heard a menacing growl. Lazarus, Lord Rakenhell's massive hound, had sniffed them out and was about to spring.

There was no time to worry
about being seen. Leaping to their
feet, Harry and Anna fled.

Harry clambered over a wall
and kept on running, down to the
misty marshes. He'd lost sight of
Anna, but the dog was close behind.

The next minute,
Harry began to sink into
the marsh. As he cried out
for help, Lazarus sprang
up and clamped his arm
between vicious fangs.

Just when Harry thought things couldn't get worse, a horrifying figure appeared.

"Let go!" the stranger shouted to Lazarus.

The dog obeyed instantly. As he trotted away, the stranger pulled a terrified Harry out of the marsh.

"Now follow me," the stranger ordered. "This marsh is dangerous. You must step exactly where I step. Do you understand?"

Harry nodded and they set off
through the mist. But they hadn't
gone far before Harry heard a
dreadful wailing. He gasped.
The boggy ground seemed to
be filled with skeletons,
which were reaching
out to grab
him...

Help me!

Chapter 6

Waking up

The next thing Harry knew, he was
waking up in a strange bed, in a
bright, warm room. Looking around
in surprise, he saw Anna grinning
at him. "Where are we?" he asked.
"How did we get here?"

"It was amazing," Anna began. "I was completely lost, when I saw the ghost of my dead mother."

"What?" cried Harry.

"I know it sounds crazy," Anna went on, "but she led me through the marshes, and then Edmund brought me here."

"Who's Edmund?" asked Harry.

She means me!

"Hello again, Harry," said a tall man, with a grin. "We've already met on the marshes, but I was covered in bandages. Ready to come down for breakfast?"

"Yes thank you, sir!" Harry said, leaping up. He liked Edmund at once. But who was he? Why did he wear bandages on his head? And how had he managed to control Lazarus?

Downstairs, Edmund put more logs on the fire. "You don't have to call me sir, Harry," he said gently. "Now I'm sure you have hundreds of questions, but let's eat first."

Edmund cooked Harry and Anna the best breakfast they had ever eaten, with plump sausages, runny eggs, crisp bacon and stacks of toast.

"Edmund?" Harry asked, when he was too full for another bite, "Why were you wearing all those bandages last night?"

"Two reasons," Edmund replied. "One, so I'm not recognized, and two, so I don't breathe in any terrible marsh gas."

Anna looked worried. "Why don't you want to be recognized?" she asked. "Have you done something *wicked*?"

Edmund spluttered into his tea. "Oh no!" he said. "I just don't want someone to know I'm here. I had to leave Nether Bogey once before because of him," he added mysteriously. "This time I mean to stay."

Chapter 7

A strange story

Harry and Anna were more
confused than ever, but Edmund
had no time for other questions.

"I'm afraid I have to go," he said,
"but I'll be back soon. You'll be safe
here." And he set off, with a scarf
wound tightly around his head.

"Did you recognize him?" Harry asked Anna, when they were alone. "I'm sure I've seen him before."

Anna shook her head. "He seems friendly though," she said.

Suddenly, there was a knock on the window and a loud scream.

They're alive!

"Miss Charlotte?" Harry dashed to the door to let her in.

"I thought you were dead," she cried, "I can't believe you're here!" Quickly, she told them what had happened at Mystery Mansion.

In the middle of last night, she had been woken by Mr. Paulfrey shouting at the servants.

"Listen all of you! Is anyone missing?" he had demanded.

Then, in the morning, Mr. Paulfrey announced that Harry and Anna had stolen a silver cup.

He said they'd dropped the cup before drowning in the marshes.

The thieves left this evidence.

But we're not thieves!

"Don't worry," said Charlotte. "My father will sort this out."

Harry took a deep breath. "It's not as simple as that," he said. "I think your father and Paulfrey are up to something together."

Chapter 8

Waking nightmares

Thora Mulch was the nosiest person in Nether Bogey. She was always asking awkward questions. Why did so many people drown in the marshes? And what had frightened Jimmy Flint?

Thora thought back to other strange events. Old Ma Gibbons had thrown herself under a cart, screaming that witch-hunters were after her.

Leave me alone!

Thomas Bradpole had drowned himself in the river, to escape from the shadows that haunted him every night.

And Magnus Duggan had broken several ribs after his dreadful fall. Now, he was being cared for at Mystery Mansion.

The village doctor was checking up on him every day...

Dr. Grimm's here to see you, again.

Now, Thora had started having nightmares too. Many years ago, her husband Norman had tripped over the cat and broken his neck. Every night, his ghost was haunting her with its neck all twisted.

Thora was terrified that she'd be the next to die.

That morning, Thora was walking into the village when she heard some footsteps close behind her. Peering through the mist, she saw a shadowy figure with a strangely twisted neck.

Oh no, not Norman!

A piercing scream rang through the air as Thora Mulch collapsed in a heap.

Chapter 9

Temper tantrum

Meanwhile, up at Mystery Mansion, Lord Rakenhell was in another furious rage. "First my son leaves me and now my daughter has disappeared," he stormed.

Throwing himself onto a tiger skin rug, he began to beat the floor with his fists.

In a few minutes, he was completely tangled up in the rug. "Get this thing off me!" he howled. "It's eating me alive!"

The housekeeper was trying to calm him down when Dr. Grimm arrived and gave Lord Rakenhell a large injection. Then he turned to the housekeeper.

"We must get him away from here as soon as we can. He can't take much more of this."

Jack O'Lantern will destroy us all.

Chapter 10

Shocks and surprises

Back at Edmund's cottage, Anna was making tea when Edmund returned – with Thora in his arms.

"Bring some water quickly!" he called to Anna.

Anna ran to the water pump.
But then she heard a cruel laugh.

If it isn't little Anna!

It was Paulfrey. "Lazarus seems
pleased to see you," he sneered. "I
think I'll let him off the leash."

Anna screamed.

The second before Lazarus
launched himself on Anna, a clear
voice rang out from the cottage.
"No boy!" cried Edmund, and
the hound slumped to the ground.

Paulfrey was furious – and very
confused. "That dog never obeys
strangers..." He looked more
closely at Edmund. "Hey! Haven't
I seen you somewhere before?"
he demanded.

Edmund smiled. "Indeed you have," he replied. "Surely you haven't forgotten me?"

Paulfrey's jaw dropped. "You're..."

Master Edmund!

"Yes Paulfrey. I'm Edmund Rakenhell!"

Harry and Charlotte, who had raced out behind Edmund, listened in amazement as he went on.

"Did you think, when you forced me to leave home ten years ago, that I was gone for good?"

"Edmund!" Charlotte interrupted, "Is it really you? Why didn't you come home to Mystery Mansion?"

"I didn't trust Paulfrey not to turn Father against me," said Edmund. "Colly knew I was back. He gave me a key to the cottage."

Edmund glared at Paulfrey. "I've come back to sort out Jack O'Lantern... and you," he declared.

"What can you do?" sneered Paulfrey. "Jack is turning all the villagers crazy – and your father, with his rages, is craziest of all!"

"And that suits you," Edmund retorted. "He's too worried about Jack to notice your bullying – or stealing."

Paulfrey's face grew bright red. He looked as if he were about to hit Edmund, but then he simply turned and ran off into the marsh.

"Paulfrey's been stealing from Father for years," Edmund told the others. "When I found out, he bullied me until I left home."

"But who's Jack?" asked Harry. "He sounds worse than Mr. Paulfrey."

"Oh, Jack O' Lantern isn't a man," said Edmund. "It's the name of the yellow gas in the marshes. When the marsh plants rot, they give off a dangerous gas that makes people see things."

"Like skeletons?" asked Harry, remembering his trip across the marsh.

"Or ghosts..." said Anna. It was all starting to make sense.

"So all the nightmares are Jack's fault," put in Charlotte.

"Exactly!" Edmund said. "Father has tried to stop it for years. I even remember him digging up plants at night to study them."

Harry and Anna looked at each other.

"So that's what he was doing by the chapel!" Anna thought.

"But why was Lord Rakenhell so secretive?" Harry asked.

"He didn't want anyone to know how dangerous the gas was," Edmund explained. "He was afraid everyone would leave and the village would die."

"But it must be the gas that's making Father's rages worse," said Charlotte. "We'll have to leave."

Edmund shook his head and smiled at her. "I've been studying the marsh plants for ten years. Last month, I finally found a plant we can grow that will destroy Jack!"

When Edmund walked through the door of Mystery Mansion, Lord Rakenhell shouted for joy. But he was even more excited when he heard his son's news.

"It's a miracle!" he cried. "After all these years... Soon the nightmares will be over forever."

What happened afterwards...

Edmund's plan to make the marsh gas harmless worked. Today, there are still mists around the house and village but they don't glow in the dark or make people see things.

Mystery Mansion was renamed Misty Mansion and became a different place. Lord Rakenhell decided to take a trip around the world. He left Edmund in charge, and the servants became the most well-treated in the country.

Harry grew up and became a butler.

Miss Charlotte married a man named Lord Snortle and had seven children.

And Edmund paid for Anna to go to college where she became an expert on plants.

As for Mr. Paulfrey — he vanished into the marsh mist and was never seen again.

A sprig of *Misteria Destroyalis*, the plant discovered by Edmund Rakehell, which now grows all over the marshes around Nether Bogey.

Series editor: Lesley Sims

Designed by
Katarina Dragoslavic

Cover design by Russell Punter

First published in 2004 by Usborne Publishing Ltd., Usborne House,
83-85 Saffron Hill, London EC1N 8RT, England. www.usborne.com
Copyright © 2004, 1995 Usborne Publishing Ltd.